July 2017

The Creole Cats are happy to share their story with the Nemer boys.

Warmly,

Mina J. Haydel

Creole Cats Come to Louisiana

Creole Cats Come to Louisiana

by Nina J. Haydel

illustrated by Diane B. Weatherby-Doorman

Instant Publisher.com

Dedication: To my husband, Belmont F. Haydel, Ph. D., the Creole inspiration for this book. –N.J.H.

Acknowledgements: Many thanks to Elinor Soll-Cohen for her New Orleans advice and to my students in the Central Michigan University Masters of Arts in Education program, who reviewed the book's content with a child's eye. I especially wish to thank my husband, Belmont Haydel, a native New Orleans Creole, for his technical advice and historical background on this subject. –N.J.H.

Dedication: To my family for their patience; to Nina J. Haydel for providing me with this opportunity; and to my former students, who have inspired me to see the world with their imagination and through their eyes. –D.B.W.D

Acknowledgements: Thanks to my friend, colleague, and professor, Nina J. Haydel for this wonderful experience and to Amanda Labadie, whose technical expertise has been invaluable in preparing this book for publication. –D.B.W.D.

Note to Readers: In the back of the book, the following can be found: Definitions for words printed in **bold** in the Glossary, historical background of French Quarter, and coloring activity.

Library of Congress Cataloging-in-Publication Data

Haydel, Nina J.

      Creole cats come to Louisiana / by Nina J. Haydel; illustrated by Diane B.

         Weatherby-Doorman

      Contents: From France to Louisiana – JoJo Adds to His Plantation - Life in New

         Orleans – Creole kitties join the family – Growing up during Mardi Gras -

         The Crab Cake Ball.

Includes parents and teachers' resources, glossary, map of the French Quarter, history of the

French Quarter, references, coloring page, recipes, related National Education Standards, web

sites.

ISBN 1-59872-582-3

1. Juvenile historical fantasy. 2. Louisiana history. 3. Creole culture. 4. Cats as

Creoles. 5. Childhood maturation. 6. Multicultural focus. 7. New Orleans Mardi Gras.

To Parents and Teachers

Creole Cats Come to Louisiana, a multicultural historical fantasy using cats to represent Creole people of Louisiana, was created to introduce a unique Louisiana culture to children in and beyond the United States' Gulf states area.

The idea was born from the book *The Victor Haydel Family: Plantation Beginnings and Early Descendants,* by Belmont F. Haydel, which serves as a genealogy of a famous Creole family (the Heidels/Haydels), dating back to the early 18th century.

The Creole culture bridges many races and mixtures of many nationalities. The term is derived from the Spanish word *criollo,* invented by a Spanish conquistador to distinguish the offsprings of European whites in Colonial Louisiana from the Native Americans and European-born settlers (Haydel, 2006). The term initially was used to designate a native Louisiana resident of pure white blood. Eventually, the meaning shifted to refer to a slave of African descent, who was born in the new world and cohabited with a white settler to produce mixed-race children (Sternberg, 2001). This Creole society has reached beyond physical and cultural boundaries to embody music, food, dancing, and architecture. Creole people come in different skin tones and ancestries.

Hence, JoJo and Mary Meow, the protagonists of the book, come to Louisiana from France and Germany, marry and produce Creole kittens with different colors of fur. These characters represent the descendants of the original French, German, and Spanish settlers, who continue to identify with the Creole culture, using the term to designate their specific group in 21st century society. These descendants, known as "Free People of Color, or *les gens de couleur libre"* define the Creole culture, today (in Haydel, 2006, by T. Delphin, p. x.).

Since the 1990s, the Louisiana Creole Heritage Center, based in Natchitoches, Louisiana, and associated with Northwestern State University of Louisiana, along with the St. Augustine Historical Society, has dedicated itself to the resurrection and preservation of Louisiana Creole culture.

The purpose of this historical fantasy, *Creole Cats Come to Louisiana,* is to provide children with awareness, clarity, and understanding of the Louisiana Creole society.

-N.J.H.-

Contents

Chapter 1

From France to Louisiana

"Oh my! What am I going to do? I'm so unhappy. All day, I plow the fields, plant vegetables, and when they grow, I pick them with my two front paws," sadly complained JoJo, who usually was a lively young cat, full of fun and laughter. "I am too sad to laugh any more. I give all my earnings to the owner of the farm, Farmer Jacques, who takes the vegetables to the market, sells them, and keeps all the money for himself. I must leave France and find a better life."

JoJo was among the many young cats that lived a long time ago in Europe, far across the Atlantic Ocean from the colonies and territories that became the United States. The cats looked for a chance to travel across the ocean to the **New World**, where they hoped to find jobs and a better life. "I want to be on my own and work for myself," said JoJo to his friend Paul, who also worked for Farmer Jacques. "I am always bending, and carrying, and Farmer Jacques makes all the money. I don't see any chance to have money for myself." "JoJo," said Paul. "I just heard about a man with a huge ship, who can take you across the Atlantic Ocean to the New World. There, you can find a place to work for yourself and have a new start. In the New World, the countries of Europe own colonies where everyone is free to work."

"Why don't you come with me? We could have a wonderful, exciting life together," replied JoJo.

"Oh, no," answered Paul. "I am afraid to change what I have been doing all these years. I am afraid of the unknown."

"Well, I'm not," shouted JoJo as he clapped his paws together. "I am ready to find my future across the ocean."

JoJo was so happy with the idea that he could start a new life. The first chance JoJo had, he went to the town near the sea. JoJo asked, "Has anybody heard about a ship going to the New World?"

"Oh, yes," replied a fellow cat. "A man by the name of **John Law** is going to sail next Monday. He is just over there, in the corner of that shop, standing by the French flag."

JoJo hurried over to the corner, his whiskers twitching and his tummy producing a purring sound. He could not stop his heart from beating wildly. "Mr. John Law, are you going to sail to the New World? I want to go with you. When do we leave?"

"My, my, young master cat, you are certainly excited. I will be happy to take you to the New World, where you can work and build a new life. Anyone as excited as you will be a success. I am sailing to a place called **Colonial Louisiana** because it is in the new continent across the ocean. It is named for King Louis of France. In Louisiana, everyone speaks French, just like they do here in France."

Come to the dock early Monday morning," and John Law pointed to where the ship was tied. "Be ready to say good-bye to all your friends and family, for you will never see them again."

JoJo felt his paws shake with fear. He had not thought of that. Leaving his home and all that he knew, never to see any of that again- this was a new idea. "What shall I do?" thought JoJo to himself. He felt as if his mind were turning upside-down. He felt as if his tummy were turning inside-out. He began to have an argument with himself.

"If I leave, I will never see my friends again. If I leave, I will never see my family again. If I leave, I will never see my farm again. All that I know will be gone, forever."

Then, the other voice inside his head answered him, "If I leave, I will find a new life. I will have new friends. I will work on a new farm that will be all mine. I will have a chance at a new life that I can build in a new world." This voice won the argument, and JoJo

prepared to travel on John Law's ship to the New World and Colonial Louisiana.

So, JoJo sold all his possessions, packed his bag with the few things he would need for the trip, and placed his money in a separate sack, careful not to lose it. He would need all the money to buy his own farm, a dream he always had.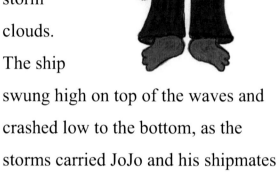

The trip was very long because the ship was very slow. Huge waves pounded the ship as rain tumbled from frequent storm clouds.

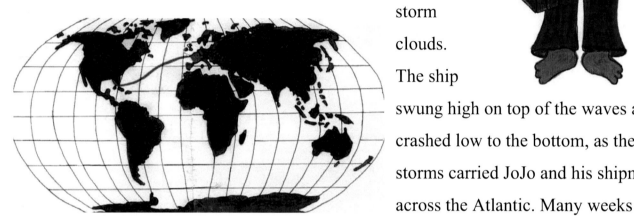

The ship swung high on top of the waves and crashed low to the bottom, as the storms carried JoJo and his shipmates across the Atlantic. Many weeks passed as the ship sailed from one shore to the other.

Sometimes, JoJo was frightened. "I think I am getting seasick. The ship is swaying like a leaf in the wind. Will it turn over?" JoJo asked the little grey cat crouched on all four paws, sitting next to him. They both used their long nails to try to hold onto the brown wooden rails that had been placed on the floor of the ship's cabin to keep the cats from sliding. The little grey cat looked up into JoJo's eyes, but did not even meow an answer. His eyes spoke for him. The cats were often terrified. They tipped from one side of the rails to the other. But, the ship never turned over and managed to ride the waves like a surfboard. John Law was a wonderful, experienced ship's captain.

Once the ship moved into the harbor, JoJo turned to his inner thoughts, "What is this new land going to look like? What are the people going to be like? Will anybody be my friend?" Worry, worry was all JoJo could do now. He could not go back.

Finally, he arrived at colonial Louisiana. Carrying his bag and sack of money, he boarded a small paddleboat and sailed up the **Mississippi River** to a tiny farming town named **LaPlace,** which means *The Place* in French. When JoJo left the ship, he looked

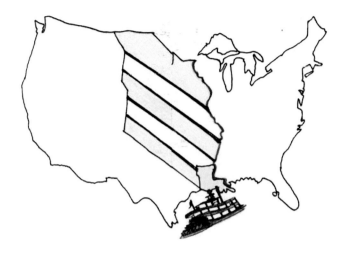

around and saw many farms available for sale. He began to plan his new life.

"I know what I will do. I will find a piece of land along this beautiful Mississippi River, and I will make my own farm here in LaPlace, Louisiana." The land he selected was very narrow across the front facing the Mississippi River, but it was very deep and long. JoJo's land became his own **plantation**. In Louisiana, big farms like this are called

Next door to JoJo's farm was another plantation. And next door to that one was another plantation. They were lined up like slices of pizza, along both sides of the Mississippi River. Every plantation was owned by a different family, who all became friends, speaking French and eating French food, just as they did before they came to Louisiana plantations.

JoJo discovered that he had nothing to fear. He thought, "I am so busy with my planting and building my new life, that I have no time to be homesick for the friends and family I left in France. I am making new friends and working hard to be a successful plantation owner."

JoJo found many workers who had also

come to Louisiana on John Law's ships, and he hired them to help build a big plantation house. JoJo lived in the house and his workers lived in small houses around the plantation.

There, he grew cotton. He was so happy working on his own land. His worker cats, called farm-paws, picked the cotton, which he took to the big city, New Orleans. There, owners of cotton gins bought the raw cotton balls. Then, the cotton gin cleaned the cotton balls and prepared the fibers for spinning into cotton thread. Factory cats wove the thread on looms and made cloth for seamstress cats to sew into dresses, shirts, suits, and hats.

JoJo worked hard on his plantation, making more and more money. He had many friends and spoke French to them. Because JoJo was very polite and very friendly, everyone liked him. But, he grew lonely living alone in the big plantation house.

"I am happy to have my own land, and I am able to work for myself. I am free to do whatever I want. I have lots of money to spend. But, none of this is fun if I have to do it alone. I wish I had someone to share my life with me." JoJo wanted a wife.

Chapter 2

JoJo Adds to His Plantation

One summer day, when the wind was breezing through the fields and the smell of cotton was in the air, JoJo visited the plantation next door. Farmer Franz grew sugar cane on his plantation. He, too, had many cats working for him. These worker farmpaws cut the cane, churned it in big pots, and separated the juice from the shuck. The juices are made into grains called sugar. The sugar was then taken to markets in New Orleans, where it was sold to be used in baking and cooking.

Farmer Franz had a big plantation house, too, surrounded by a long porch around the front and sides of the house. There were white rocking chairs lined up on the front porch and long stairs that swirled around the side of the house. The wind played with the empty white chairs, making them rock and rock, back and forth.

JoJo climbed the porch stairs that led to the front door. He knocked his paw against the door, and it swung open. **"*Bon jour*,"** said JoJo to his neighbor, Farmer Franz, who stood behind the door. That means *hello* or *good day* in French. Farmer Franz had come to Louisiana from Germany, but he now spoke French, too. "I am your neighbor who grows cotton over there." JoJo pointed in the direction of his land.

"*Bon jour,*" answered Farmer Franz. "Please come and sit on my porch. I am happy to finally meet you. Would you like some milk to drink?"

"Yes, thank you," answered JoJo, and he sat in the smallest white rocker overlooking the twisted stairs.

Farmer Franz called to his daughter to bring large bowls of cold, sweet cow's milk for them to drink. The day was cool, as the huge oak trees fluttered over the porch to share the breeze with the cats sitting nearby. JoJo looked at the cat that carefully climbed the stairs from the kitchen on the bottom floor to the porch above. She balanced two bowls of milk on a blue glass tray in her delicate paws. JoJo could not believe his eyes. Here appeared the most beautiful grey, black, and white cat he had ever seen. "*Bon jour,*" said JoJo, as he caught his breath and felt his heart tingle. "Who is that?" JoJo asked Farmer Franz.

"That is my daughter, Mary Meow."

"I would like to get to know Mary Meow," said JoJo. "May I have your permission to see her, if she is willing?"

Farmer Franz snuck a smile at the corners of his mouth, nodded his head and said, "I will be very happy for you to get to know my daughter. She is a wonderful **seamstress** and can sew better than any cats in LaPlace, Louisiana." He liked the idea of Mary Meow meeting a nice young male cat, who could make her happy. She was often lonely on her plantation, too.

Mary Meow looked at JoJo with soft eyes that came to rest on his face like a butterfly on a flower. She knew JoJo was the right one for her. Her sweet meows were the music that made JoJo happy.

JoJo's heart danced in his chest, for he had found his love, Mary Meow. After a short time of getting to know each other better, Mary Meow told JoJo, "I will be happy to be your wife." Now, he had a best friend who spoke French to him and made him very content. He sang to her and gave her many lovely gifts, dolls made of cotton, bracelets made of oyster shells, candies called **pralines**, made of honey and nuts.

JoJo thought to himself, "How could I have ever been frightened about coming to the New World. My life is very full, now. I am glad I had the courage to make a change in my life."Mary Meow and JoJo got married on the plantation. They had a wonderful wedding with all the Mississippi neighboring cats as guests. Music and food surrounded the wedding party, very much like the cats had enjoyed in France. Everyone was joyful for the bride and groom.

Mary Meow moved into JoJo's plantation house. She helped him manage all his farmpaw workers, who

grew and picked the cotton from the plants in the fields. They continued to send the raw cotton balls by wagons to the New Orleans marketplace. The cats that bought the cotton would sew it into hats, jackets, pants, and skirts, then sell the items in the shops along the main streets of the city.

JoJo and Mary Meow were happy, although they worked very

hard. JoJo got up early in the morning, working side-by-side with his paw hands, all day until the sun went down and the night began to cover them. Then, he would help load the horse-driven wagons to market. Mary Meow worked at his side and also supervised the female cats, which cooked the food for all the paw hands and took care of the large plantation house.

One day, Mary Meow said, "I am tired. I want to find an easier life than farming cotton and cooking for all those cats on the plantation. I would like to go to **New Orleans**, live there, and open a shop to sell things. I am a **superb** seamstress, and I can make dolls out of cotton and straw. Let us move to the big city."

JoJo again heard his inner voice arguing. "I am happy here, although the work is very hard. I have a beautiful plantation house, much land to grow my cotton crops, and many friends. I will have to leave all that I know to start over in a new place."

His other voice took charge of his thoughts and said, "How exciting it will be to have another adventure. I will be able to start something new and see it build into a success. I do not have to leave my family, for Mary Meow will be at my side. I can even travel to visit my old friends in LaPlace. I will move."

After JoJo agreed to the changes in their lives, they sold the plantation to a new cat that had just arrived from France. JoJo told the new owner, "Do not be afraid of this great change in your life. It is an adventure. Enjoy every moment of it."

So, Mary Meow and JoJo, with the help of Farmer Franz, packed their wagons and went to New Orleans.

Chapter 3

Life in New Orleans

In New Orleans, JoJo and Mary Meow arrived at a special area called the **French Quarter**. Everybody there spoke French, too, just like on the plantations.

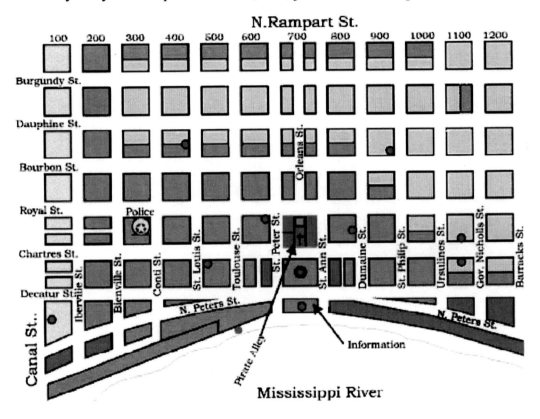

http://www..atneworleans.com/body/map-fq.htm

The French Quarter had lots of shops, restaurants, and houses built with iron balconies that hugged the top floors. Cats could climb on the iron railings, sit with their tails delicately hanging through the bars, and look at the road below, watching all the other cats purring along the streets. The unusual buildings attracted many cats that came from far and near to shop, eat, and enjoy the sights of the famous city, New Orleans.

JoJo and Mary Meow found a house on **Bourbon Street** that had a huge balcony around the top floor. Mary Meow said to JoJo, "We can have the top floor as our home. It has a living room, dining room, kitchen, and bedrooms all on the top floor. We even have room for kittens someday. On the first floor, we can set up the cotton gin to spin the cotton into thread. Then, we must hire cats to weave the cotton into cloth. I will teach them how to sew in order to create our dolls." That's just what they did!

Every morning, JoJo and Mary Meow would go down to the factory in the back of the first floor under their home. In the factory the paw-workers sewed the cotton material into very special dolls, called YOO-DOO dolls, which Mary Meow sold in their store in the front of the first floor.

Throughout New Orleans many striped cats, polka dot cats, black and white cats, brown cats, tabby cats, and grey cats had been talking about the YOO-DOO dolls made in the house with the long black balcony on Bourbon Street. JoJo and Mary-Meow became very well known for these paw-made dolls. JoJo created the design for the dolls. The body and arms of the dolls were made of straw, all wrapped round and round in colorful cotton outfits that Mary Meow and the paw-workers sewed. The head of the dolls was made of a round piece of wood.

JoJo painted the head black and drew eyes, a nose, and a mouth on the wood. On top of the head, Mary Meow tied the ends of the straw in a scarf. The straw looked like hair. The dolls were believed to have a special use: to tell the owners what to do to be happier, healthier and successful in life.

All the cats thought the dolls could help them do what they needed to do. In the minds of the owners of the dolls, the dolls would say, "You do this: Go home and help your family clean the house. You do this: Go to the market and help the old cats carry their packages. You do this: Go to school and listen to the teacher, so you can learn how to read and write. You do this: Go to Grandma's house in the country today and help her do her chores." Many decisions were made according to the YOO-DOO dolls' influence, or so the cats thought.

New Orleans cats came to the store to buy these special dolls because they wanted to be able to do all their work very well. They wanted the dolls to help them decide to do the right thing in all circumstances. Many kittens were keeping YOO-DOO dolls in their backpacks when they went to school. They wanted the dolls to help them do their homework too.

Mary Meow sold the dolls from the counter in the store, and JoJo delivered many of them in his little truck to other French families in New Orleans. The YOO-DOO dolls were making JoJo and Mary Meow famous. Cats came from all parts of Louisiana to buy the YOO-DOO dolls, hoping that the dolls would help them decide what to do in their lives.

Chapter 4

Creole Kitties Join the Family

JoJo and Mary Meow's own personal YOO-DOO doll helped them decide to have a family. Mary Meow told JoJo, "We have a wonderful home in the French Quarter and a successful business with our YOO-DOO dolls. Now it is time for us to bring new kittens into the world."

So, they prepared a nursery for their Creole kittens. Before long, Mary Meow had five little kitties. All their friends came to see Mary Meow and JoJo with their Creole kittens. "Thank you, YOO-DOO doll, for now we have a lovely family," said JoJo.

The new little kitties are called **Creole** kitties because JoJo came from France, and these are the first kitties of this French family to be born in Louisiana.

Everyone who had come from France, Spain, and Germany and settled in Louisiana had Creole babies. That special name told the world these kitties were born in Louisiana and had parents from countries in Europe, across the Atlantic Ocean.

JoJo and Mary Meow had five Creole kitties. JoJo was a brown cat. Mary Meow was a grey, black, and white cat. Their kitties were many different colors. JimJim was white. JayJay was grey. BoBo was brown. SueSue was black. LeeLee was black and white with pink ears.

JimJim

JayJay

BoBo

LeeLee

SueSue

They were a Creole cat family of many different colors that loved to play with the cotton that Mary Meow sewed to make the clothes for the YOO-DOO dolls she sold in the store.

JoJo and Mary Meow took good care of their Creole kitties. Every morning, the kitties would wake up in their little bed,

take a bath,

brush their teeth,

and eat breakfast.

One morning, as the kitties were getting ready for school, LeeLee asked his mother, "MaMa, why are we all different colors? JayJay is grey, and BoBo is brown? SueSue is black, but JimJim is white. Look at me!"

Mary Meow stopped brushing the fur on LeeLee's ears, which was almost pink on the black crown of fur covering his white face. She gathered her kittens around her and told them, "You are all different colors because PaPa and I have different color fur. PaPa is brown and I am grey. You are a part of each one of us and of the cats who were our mamas and papas. You are Creoles because you are born in Louisiana, and PaPa was born in France. I was born in Germany. Someday, you will grow up and have your own kittens. They, too, will be Creoles with fur of many different colors."

The Creole kitties listened carefully and began to understand why they all looked different and were known as Creole cats. Then, they went off to school.

In New Orleans, Creole kitties did not go to the same school as other kitties that were not born from families who once lived in Europe. The five kitties went to a Creole school with other Creole kitties, also born in Louisiana. Some of the kitties had parents who came from France, Africa, Spain and Germany, other countries far across the Atlantic Ocean. Some parents were **Native American** cats. All these kitties were called Creoles, regardless of the color of their fur.

Chapter 5

Let the Good Times Roll

As JoJo and Mary Meow watched their Creole kitties grow older, they began to worry. JoJo often said to Mary Meow, "Our kitties have no worries, happily having fun and good times every day, here in New Orleans. When I was a young cat in France, I had to work in the fields for Farmer Jacques, even when I was a kitten. Our kitties are becoming young cats, yet they have no idea about what they would do when they would grow up. They cannot stay kitties forever. All they want to do is play and *let the good times roll.*"

"I know what you mean," answered Mary Meow. "They love to go to the beach in **Mississippi**, the state next door to Louisiana, and sit in the sun.

"I often look down through the iron bars of the balcony and see them ride their bicycles through the streets of the French Quarter.

"I know they dream of skating all around New Orleans. Sometimes they put little wheels on two paws to slide down Bourbon Street.

"Sometimes they would even ride their motorcycles down Canal Street and throughout the French Quarter.

"Sometimes they would take the canoe and paddle on a narrow, deep canal, **Bayou St. John**.

"Sometimes they go to the **Gulf of Mexico** near the ships, and they fish. All they want to do is play."

The Creole kitties would shout, "*Let the good times roll*," and not think about what they would be able to do when they would grow up and be Creole Cats, just like JoJo and Mary Meow. *Let the good times roll* became their favorite saying and a famous saying, till this day, in southern Louisiana.

Chapter 6

Growing Up During Mardi Gras

There were many celebrations in New Orleans, and the Creoles cats loved parades. One of the most famous was the **Mardi Gras** parade. Mardi Gras is a French name that means **Fat Tuesday**. The special parade was held on Tuesday, while the people of New Orleans partied and ate. Some got very fat, too.

On Mardi Gras, JoJo and Mary Meow called all the kittens together before they left home to see the Mardi Gras parade that snakes through the French Quarter.

Mary Meow and JoJo were very worried about their kitties, who only wanted to play. Now that the kitties were getting older, JoJo wanted them to plan their future when they would grow into cats. Of course, they would not stay kittens forever.

Mary Meow told them, "Now that you are getting older, you can have a YOO-DOO doll that will help you decide what is best for you to do. The doll will help you plan what you will do in the future. You cannot play and play all the time. You must get ready to grow up."

SueSue said, "We don't want to grow up, MaMa. We do not know what we will do when we get older, and we do not care. But, we will take our YOO-DOO dolls with us to the Mardi Gras parade."

As the sun danced on the rivers and bayous, all the young Creole cats dressed in fancy costumes, put masks over their eyes, arranged their whiskers, and marched behind the big parade that went round and round the streets in New Orleans, from Bayou St. John to **City Park**, to the Mississippi River.

Suddenly, as the five Creole kitties were bouncing along, LeeLee shouted, "My YOO-DOO doll is telling me to do something." Many puddles covered the road because many restaurants emptied their extra food and pots into the streets. Just that fast, LeeLee fell into a huge pudding puddle. When he picked himself up, he was covered in the most delicious chocolate pudding. The other kitties began to lick his fur, not just to clean him, but to eat the wonderful tasting pudding. LeeLee took out his YOO-DOO doll, held it high in the air and shouted, "Now, I know what you want me to do. I will grow up and become a Creole cook. I may even open a Creole restaurant."

All the kitties clapped their paws, for LeeLee would learn to cook **gumbo** (a special Louisiana soup), and **jambalaya** (a special chicken or seafood stew), **crawfish étouffé**, (a special rice and crawfish stew), and sauces with spices too delicious to imagine.

BoBo looked at LeeLee and responded very sadly, "I do not know what my YOO-DOO doll wants me to do, but yours has told you." BoBo closed his eyes and looked inside himself, as he saw the backs of his eyelids. "I am never as good as my sister and brother. They can do more than I do in school; they can ride better than I do on their bikes; they can run faster than I do in the street. I never feel as good as they do."

"You will have your turn soon, I am sure," answered LeeLee, not realizing the sadness BoBo felt.

The Creole kitties continued following the Mardi Gras parade down **Royal Street** in the French Quarter. They looked at all the floats with cats in costumes riding in wagons decorated with paper flowers. Some Mardi Gras cats dressed as clowns threw strings of beads to the kitties watching the parade. Paws reached out for the beads and swung them around their neck. Music floated from the bands that marched behind the floats. The air had a smoky shimmer to it, as the sun multiplied the heat of a New Orleans day.

Suddenly, SueSue felt something besides the beads falling on her head. It was a beautiful magnolia blossom. Someone was throwing flowers from a balcony above. SueSue reached into her pocket and pulled out her YOO-DOO doll and said, "Now, I know what you want me to do. I will open a flower shop and sell sweet smelling flowers to all the people in New Orleans."

All the kitties clapped their paws, for SueSue would learn to make fancy bouquets of flowers for brides at their wedding, and pots of flowers to decorate New Orleans' houses.

BoBo once again felt that he could not do anything right. He looked at SueSue and sadly responded, "I do not know what my YOO-DOO doll wants me to do, but yours has told you."

"You will have your turn soon, I am sure," answered SueSue, not realizing the sadness BoBo felt.

The Mardi Gras parade turned down **Canal Street**, and the Creole kitties continued dancing along with the parade.

Suddenly, JayJay, who was not watching where he was going, walked into a pole. He grabbed his cheek and meowed at the top of his voice, for he had hurt his face. As the hurt grew less, he meowed softer and softer. His voice went high and low, high and low, as he cried and cried. His YOO-DOO doll suddenly fell out of his pocket. JayJay looked at it, wiped away his tears, and said, "I know what the YOO-DOO doll wants me to do, to become a singer. I will sing for everyone of New Orleans. They will come to hear me sing from all around Louisiana." All the kitties

36

clapped their paws, for JayJay would become a famous singer and sing French songs called **ballads** and sad songs called the **Blues**.

BoBo, feeling worse and worse, looked at JayJay and responded, "I do not know what my YOO-DOO doll wants me to do, but yours has told you."

"You will have your turn soon, I am sure," answered JayJay, not realizing the sadness BoBo felt.

The kitties continued to follow the parade, stepping here and there in time to the music, nobody watching where he or she was going.

JimJim suddenly stumbled and almost fell. He had stepped on top of an alligator that had climbed out of the bayou and was also following the parade.

"Oops, Mr. Alligator, I am sorry that I stepped on your back. I think I have hurt you." Just then, JimJim's YOO-DOO doll fell on Mr. Alligator's head.

"Ouch," cried Mr. Alligator. "I am really hurt, now."

"My YOO-DOO doll just told me what to do," shouted JimJim. I am going to be an animal doctor, **a veterinarian**, and make sure all the bayou animals are safe and healthy." So JimJim rubbed the alligator's back and head with his soft, furry paw.

Mr. Alligator was so happy he began to sing:

"Creole kittens, thanks so much,

For your gentle, kindly touch.

I feel better, I must say,

So I will go along my way."

All the kitties clapped their paws, for JimJim would become a famous animal doctor and cure many sick animals.

BoBo looked at JimJim, more upset than ever and responded, "I do not know what my YOO-DOO doll wants me to do, but yours has told you."

"You will have your turn soon, I am sure," answered JimJim not realizing the sadness BoBo felt.

The Creole kitties followed the **floats** down to the **levee**, a high wall that was built to keep the lake water and Mississippi River out of the streets of New Orleans. Some floats were covered with flowers; others had animals figures made of balloons and **Papier Mâché**. They were colorful and excited all the visitors and residents of New Orleans.

New Orleans is surrounded on many sides by levees. The city is built below the sea and the high levees keep it safe and dry when there are heavy rain storm called hurricanes. New Orleans looks almost like soup bowl, with the levees as the sides of the bowl and the city streets as the bottom of the bowl.

BoBo climbed up on top of the levee and began to sob, "All of you kitties have found what you are going to do when you grow up. My YOO-DOO doll is not working. It has not told me what to do when I become a big cat. I feel terrible!" Inside his head he continued thinking, "I am not as good as my sister and brothers. I will have nothing to tell MaMa and PaPa when we see them. They will love LeeLee, SueSue, JayJay, and JimJim more than they love me." His heart almost drowned in sadness.

"Please do not be sad, BoBo," said SueSue. "Your YOO-DOO doll will help you if you just let it."

"Look, everyone, there is a show going on near the levee. Let's go to the theater and see it," said JimJim.

All the Creole kitties joined many other big cats and kittens to watch the show. Dancers were performing and the music was loud and exciting. "What is that music I hear," asked BoBo? "I never heard that before."

"That is a very unique kind of music and dancing called **Zydeco**, which is very special for the Creoles of Louisiana," said an older mama cat who had overheard BoBo's question. "We all dance to that music and sing the words in a special type of French."

"I love that sound," exclaimed BoBo, who started to dance to the Zydeco music. Just then, his YOO-DOO doll fell out of his pocket. "Look, SueSue, JayJay, JimJim and LeeLee. My YOO-DOO doll is telling me what I will do: become a musician and play Zydeco music, so all the Creole cat families will be able to dance.

I will play **jazz,** another kind of music, on the saxophone, just like the musicians in the Mardi Gras parade," added BoBo, and he pretended to play a horn.

The Creole kitties clapped their paws and hugged and kissed BoBo, for now, his YOO-DOO doll had told him what to do when he grow up. BoBo was joyful! He and his sister and brother kitties could hardly wait to tell their parents, JoJo and Mary Meow, the good news about their future plans.

Chapter 7

The Crab Cake Ball

At the very same time the five Creole kitties were outside following the parade, JoJo and Mary Meow, dressed in their Mardi Gras costumes, put on their masks, and traveled to Canal Street, where they met their friends.

All the Creole cats belonged to their own Mardi Gras club, The Crab Cake Creole Club. Every year, on Fat Tuesday, after the Mardi Gras parade, the Creole parents met in an auditorium on Canal Street, to celebrate at the Crab Cake Ball. The club members wore masks, carried streamers, and held sparklers, as they greeted JoJo and Mary Meow.

"*Bon jour,*" said JoJo, as he waved his sparkler.

"*Bon jour*," said Mary Meow, as she waved her sparkler. Both JoJo and Mary Meow said hello in French.

"*Bon jour,*" answered all the other Creole cats, and they waved their sparklers, too. The twinkling lights looked like a room full of lightening bugs on a dark summer's night. This special party was called a ball because everyone was dressed in fancy clothes.

The musicians in the orchestra began to play elegant music, not jazz or Zydeco, and the Creole cats moved on to the open floor where they swayed and danced.

Waiter cats carried trays of Creole **meat pies**, **crab cakes**, **shrimp Creole**, spicy ribs, and **black- eyed peas**, all the food the cats loved. The desserts included pecan pies, banana pudding, French apple pie, pralines, and Louisiana Creole pecan candy. Atop a huge gold tray sat the **Mardi Gras Cake**, complete with green, gold, and purple icing, a feast for the eyes and the tummies.

After a while, a large black cat wearing a huge black top hat came on the stage next to the orchestra. He declared, "We are going to announce the winner of the contest we have at every Mardi Gras ball. The winner becomes the King of the Mardi Gras for the Crab Cake Club. He is a cat that has done the most, this year, to help all the Creole Cats."

"Who can that be?" asked Mary Meow. "Who has done something special enough to receive such a high honor?"

Every cat in the auditorium grew silent. No one purred or meowed. The drummer beat the drum loudly, to get everyone's attention. The Top Hat Cat raised his paw and said, "The new King of the Crab Cake Ball is…………JoJo from New Orleans."

Every cat clapped his and her paws and shouted, "Hurrah for JoJo."

The Top Hat Cat announced, "JoJo has done something special for all of the Creoles. He and Mary Meow have created and sold YOO-DOO dolls to all the Creole cats. These dolls help us decide what to do about our lives and our families. Because of the YOO-DOO dolls, we always know the right thing to do. We make the right decisions." Top Hat Cat handed the King's **scepter** to JoJo. Then, he placed the King's robe around JoJo's shoulders and put the King's crown on his head. "Thank you JoJo for helping us. Thank you Mary Meow for helping JoJo."

Just then, the five kittens arrived at the ball. They had finished following the parade and wanted to visit their parents at the ball. They heard their daddy being honored as King of the Crab Cake Ball. They clapped their little paws and **beamed** with their whiskers standing straight up in the air and their purring music rising from their tummies. "How proud we are," glowed SueSue. "Not only did PaPa do something wonderful for all the other cats, but he helped us, too."

LeeLee ran to his parents and said, "We all have learned our futures from the YOO-DOO dolls you gave us. This all happened while we were parading through the streets. My YOO-DOO doll helped me decide to be a Creole chef. I will open a restaurant and sell the most delicious French Creole food in all of New Orleans."

JayJay moved next to JoJo and said, "MaMa, PaPa, my YOO-DOO doll helped me decide to become a singer. I will sing songs of the South and of Louisiana. I will sing French songs and sad songs called the Blues."

JimJim next grabbed Mary Meow's paw and said, "MaMa, my YOO-DOO doll helped me decide that I will become a veterinarian, and I will treat all the alligators and snakes that live in the bayous around New Orleans."

SueSue was next. She handed JoJo the beautiful magnolia blossom that had hit her on her head. She said, "PaPa, I will grow the most wonderful flowers that smell fragrant and beautiful. Then, I will open a flower shop and sell them to all the cats in New Orleans."

Finally, BoBo, who had been waiting behind the other kittens, smiled broadly and did a little hopping dance on his rear paws. A purring sound, like an electric motor, grew louder and louder from his tummy. "I am going to be a musician. I will play the saxophone, guitar and banjo, so everyone can hear Zydeco and jazz. I will even write songs for JayJay to sing." He knew in his heart that his parents loved him so much, even if he had not found his future.

Mary Meow smiled happily and reached her front paws out to hug all five. "PaPa and I are so proud that you could make the important decisions about your lives. You all may change your minds sometime in the future, but for now, you have an idea that will help you find the path to growing up."

Then, she looked at JoJo and said to him, "I am proud of you, JoJo, for creating YOO-DOO dolls that helped everyone decide what to do." JoJo's face beamed and his eyes sparkled like stars in a dark sky. His kittens were growing up and his work was appreciated. He was a very satisfied papa and cat.

JoJo's Creole cat family had come a long way from the time JoJo met John Law and arrived in Louisiana from France. Life in New Orleans was very happy for all the Creole cats, young and old, as the Creole kittens got ready to become young Creole cats.

Glossary

Vocabulary and Names

bayou - (pronounced *by you*) is a small, fairly shallow muddy stream that twists and turns along the southern parts of Louisiana. It is usually full of snakes and alligators.

beamed – a warm, bright, smiling expression.

bon jour – (pronounced *bon zhoor*) French for hello, a greeting.

Creole – (pronounced *kree ole*) descended from the original French settlers of Louisiana, usually of mixed European, American Indian and Negro ancestors.

farm-paws – cat farmhands working on the plantations.

Fat Tuesday – The English translation of Mardi Gras, the Tuesday before the Catholic holiday (feast day) of Ash Wednesday.

floats – Large flat boards on wheels, decorated with flowers and figures. Different groups or Mardi Gras clubs have members dressed in costumes, who ride on the floats and throw colored beads and other charms to the people on the streets.

John Law – Owner of "Company of the Indies," who operated ocean-going ships that carried Europeans to populate the New World.

Let the good times roll. – a common saying in New Orleans where people love to have fun.

levee – a raised portion of land made by people to prevent a river or other body of water from flooding lower land.

Mardi Gras – (pronounced *Mar dee Gra*) French for "Fat Tuesday." The celebration came to the U. S. Gulf Coast area with the earliest French settlers in the late 17th century and early 18th century. Iberville and Bienville LeMoyne were sent by King Louis XIV of France to defend the French claim to the territory of Louisiana. It is a carnival that occurs before the Catholic season of Lent (Mardi Gras).

Native American – An American Indian born on American soil, even before it became America.

papier mâché – (pronounced *paper ma shay*) material made of paper mixed with oil. When it is wet, it can be molded into various shapes or objects,

plantation – a large farm in the South, usually cultivated by workers who live on the farm. Every plantation has a big house (called the mansion), where the plantation owner and his family live.

seamstress – a woman whose job is sewing.

scepter – a fancy short stick held by a king to represent his ruling over his subjects.

superb – excellent, extremely fine.

veterinarian – a doctor whose patients are sick animals.

Louisiana and Southern Places

Bayou St. John – a bayou that flows throughout the northern part of New Orleans.

Bourbon Street – (pronounced **bur bun**) a main street in the New Orleans French Quarter.

Canal Street – a main street in New Orleans bordering the French Quarter that divides uptown from downtown.

City Park – main section of New Orleans located at the northern part of the city. Today, it is a huge park with a beautiful museum.

Colonial Louisiana - territory of Louisiana before the Louisiana Purchase in 1803.

French Quarter – section of New Orleans that served as the Creole center for business and fun. It is about 12 square blocks large and has been restored to its early beauty.

Gulf Coast – the states around the Gulf of Mexico.

LaPlace – (pronounced **la plah s**) small city located about 40 miles northwest of New Orleans, along the Mississippi River.

Mississippi – U. S. state, with Louisiana to its west and Alabama and Florida to its east.

Mississippi River – one of the U.S.'s largest rivers running north and south, emptying into the Gulf of Mexico. It is a major river for ships to transport goods.

New Orleans – major city in southern Louisiana, in which the French Quarter is a tourist area today.

New World – all of South America, the Caribbean Islands, Mexico, Canada, and the area that became the United States.

Royal Street – a major street in the New Orleans French Quarter, closer to the river than Bourbon Street.

Louisiana Music

ballads – a song that tells a story and usually repeats short stanzas.

blues – a kind of southern American Black folk song that usually has a sad feeling and slow rhythm. It began on southern plantations.

jazz – a kind of southern American Black music with different tones from musical horns. It began in southern Louisiana by Black musicians.

Zydeco – (pronounced **z' eye de ko**) a kind of fast folk music that began in south-west Louisiana in the 20th century by French Creole people. The music was influenced by French Cajuns and African Americans. Zydeco is usually played with a piano accordion, a form of washboard, known as a rub-board, drums, and guitar. The term Zydeco is French for *the beans,* and was first used in 1965 (Zydeco).

Louisiana Food

black-eyed peas – a medium size bean that is pale in color and has a black spot that looks like an eye. It is used in many Louisiana recipes.

crab cakes – crab meat mixed with seasoning and bread crumbs, then browned on top of the stove into patties.

crawfish – little lobster-like seafood found in rivers and lakes in southern Louisiana.

étouffé – (pronounced **ā two fay**) the name means "smothered" (Lagasse) or stewed, which refers to food cooked in its own juices or other liquids. It is made with shrimp or crawfish.

51

gumbo – thick, spicy soup made with oysters, fish, shellfish, sausage, chicken, meat and vegetables. Sometimes people cook it with just one or two of the ingredients; sometimes it is a combination of many. It is served over rice.

jambalaya – (pronounced **jum ba lie ya**) chicken, sausage, or fish browned using onions and sometimes tomatoes, then cooked with rice.

Mardi Gras cake – large cake with yellow, green, and purple icing, decorated with beads and masks. It is the centerpiece for the Mardi Gras balls. Haydel Bakery in New Orleans is famous for these cakes.

meat pies – meat-filled pie covered on both sides with dough. They are thought to have been developed by the **Natchitoches** Indians (pronounced **nack i tosh)** and were often sold from carts pushed along the streets (Lagasse, 1996).

pralines – (pronounced **praw-leens**) sweet candy made with pecans and sugar. These were originally sold in the streets of the French Quarter of Colonial Louisiana, especially around Christmas time, and were often used as rewards when children were good.

shrimp creole – shrimp cooked in a tomato sauce, then served over rice.

History of the French Quarter

Historical Background of the French Quarter

Founding: The French Quarter of New Orleans was founded in 1718 by Jean Baptiste Bienville, a French military naval officer. He was French Canadian and served as governor for John Law, the man who owned the ships that carried people from France to the Louisiana territory. The town was set up in a grid of 70 squares and followed a French plan which included a center square, known today as Jackson Square. The town also housed a church of St. Louis, a convent that educated women, and a charity hospital. This was a colony of France under King Louis XV. The residents were Europeans, slaves from Africa, and a new group of people known as Creoles, both white and free people of color.

Spanish Rule: In 1762, King Louis XV gave the French Quarter, as a gift, to his cousin Charles III of Spain. The French people in the colony were so upset that in 1768, they revolted against the Spanish. The French failed and the Spanish ruled the colony for about 40 years. As a result, much of the Spanish architecture and cooking is still enjoyed in the French Quarter. The beautiful wrought iron balconies on the buildings and the cooking with olive oil are directly related to the Spanish rule. Two great fires occurred, one in 1788 and the other in 1794. The town hall, the priests' residence, and the "French Market" remained as a major center of the French Quarter.

In 1800, Napoleon Bonaparte of France, who had conquered Europe, returned Louisiana to the French, but this was kept a secret. It took three years for the Louisiana territory to become free of the Spanish rule.

Louisiana Purchase: The City of New Orleans controlled the Mississippi River. The Americans, under Thomas Jefferson, needed the Mississippi River for shipping. In 1803, President Thomas Jefferson bought the Louisiana territory from the French in an action known as the Louisiana Purchase. He paid about 3 cents an acre for an area of more than 529,911,681 acres. The total amount of the purchase was $15 million. If this happened in 2003, it would have cost America about $390 billion. The land then was much larger than Louisiana is today. It covered all or some parts of the states of Arkansas, Missouri, Iowa, Minnesota, North Dakota, South Dakota, Nebraska, New Mexico, Northern Texas, Oklahoma, Kansas, parts of Montana, Wyoming, Colorado, sections of what is now Canada, and, of course, Louisiana on both sides of the Mississippi River. That purchase added a huge part of land to the United States. Thus, the Louisiana Purchase transferred the French colony to the United States.

The French Quarter grew as cotton, sugar, and food products traveled back and forth by steamboats up and down the Mississippi River. Americans, Irish, German, African, and French from France all found their way to this booming new area. They brought their culture, language, religion, architecture, clothing styles, and foods. Creoles were at the base of the population of the French Quarter.

Civil War and Reconstruction: The streets of the French Quarter were part of the Civil War battleground, and the town square was no longer the center of activity. Creoles moved to other parts of Louisiana, and immigrants from Sicily moved into the French Quarter. Black musicians created jazz and ragtime; writers and artists created stories about the people of this very special part of the south.

Modern Times: The French Quarter has been restored and preserved to return it to the character of the Old Quarter in the days before it became part of the United States (Reeves).

References

Adorama at New Orleans. Retrieved on 8/29/06 from

    http://ateneworleans.com/body/map-fq.htm

Chase, L. (2003). *And still I cook.* Gretna, Louisiana: Pelican Publishing.

French Quarter maps. Retricved on July 31, 2006 from French Quarter.com: maps

Haydel, B.F. (2006). *The Victor Haydel Creole family: Plantation beginnings and early*

    descendants (Unpublished manuscript). Newtown, Pennsylvania: Bucks Digital

    Printing Co.

Lagasse, E. & Bienvenu, M. (1996). *Louisiana real and rustic.* New York: William

    Morrow and Co.

Mardi Gras. Retrieved on 7/28/06 from http://en.wikipedia.org/wiki/mardigras

Prudhomme, Enola. (1991). *Enola Prudhommes low calorie Cajun cooking.* New York:

    William Morrow and Co.

Reeves, S. *Brief history of the French Quarter.* Retrieved 7/28/06 from

    http://www.inetours.com/New_Orleans/French_Quarter_History.html

Sternberg, M.A. (1996). *Along the River Road—Past and present on Louisiana historic*

    byways. Baton Rouge: Louisiana State University Press.

Zydeco. Retrieved on 7/28/06 from http://en.wikipedia.org/wiki/Zydeco

Coloring Page

Mardi Gras Mask
Color and Cut

    1. Cut out mask and glue to cardboard then cut it out again, be sure to cutout the eyes.
    2. Decorate mask by coloring with crayons, paint or markers and be sure to add glitter, feathers and ribbon.
    3. Attach mask to a straw or stick.

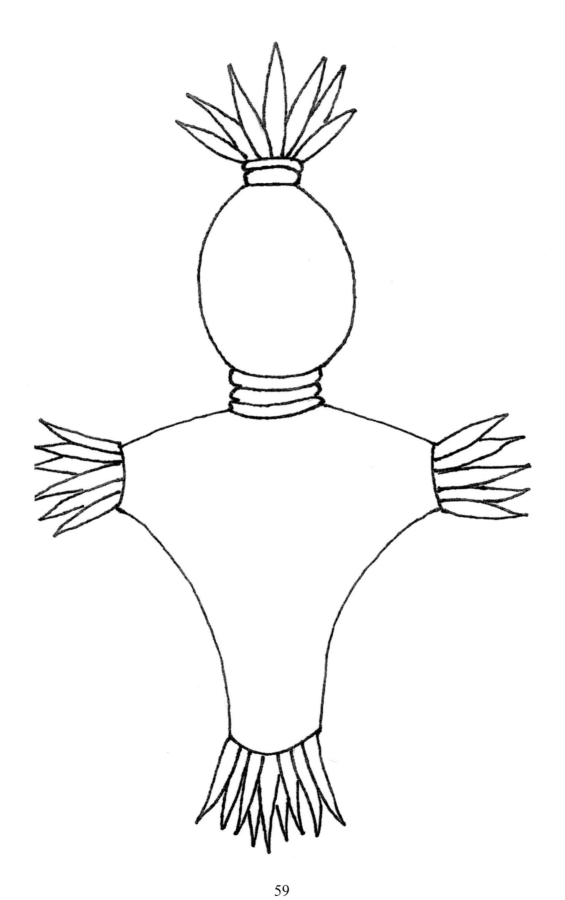

59

Mary Meow's Recipes

Louisiana Pralines: These are the candies the Creole Kittens ate while they followed the Mardi Gras Parade.

Ingredients

1 ⅓ cup sugar

⅔ cup brown sugar

1 ⅓ cup water

⅛ teaspoon salt

2 cups of pecans (Some can be broken up into pieces. Mary Meow leaves some whole.)

1. Put all the ingredients , but NOT the NUTS, in a pot and bring them to a boil.

2. Cover the pot with a lid and simmer the sugar, salt, and water on a low fire for about 3 minutes.

3. After 3 minutes, uncover the pot and continue cooking until the mixture looks like a it could become a soft ball.

4. Let the entire mixture sit and cool until it is about 110 degrees. Check the temperature with a cooking thermometer.

5. With a hand beater or electric hand mixer, beat the entire softened, cooled mixture until it gets thick and loses its shiny, glossy appearance.

6. Drop in the nuts and make sure they are spread through the entire mixture.

7. With a table spoon, drop the praline mixture onto waxed paper.

8. Let them cool completely.

9. You can wrap them individually and save them to take to school in your lunch bag.

Don't eat too many at a time, or you will get a tummy ache. BoBo can tell you how bad that feels!

(Mary Meow thanks Uncle Butsy Haydel, of New Orleans [1912-2005], for this recipe. Uncle Butsy (Honoré) was born on the Haydel Plantation that JoJo bought when he came from France.)

Creole Pecan Pie : This is one of the desserts served at the Crab Cake Ball during the Mardi Gras celebration. Each pie serves 8 people.

Ingredients

> 2 eggs
>
> ⅓ cup sugar
>
> 5½ ounces Karo dark corn syrup
>
> ⅔ teaspoon vanilla
>
> ⅓ teaspoon salt
>
> 1½ cups of chopped pecans
>
> ⅔ Tablespoon Kahlua or coffee liqueur (for parents, only) or strong coffee
>
> ⅓ Tablespoon pancake syrup
>
> ⅓ cup seedless golden raisins
>
> 1 9" unbaked pie shell (NOT deep dish pie shell)

1. Beat the eggs slightly.

2. Add the sugar, corn syrup, salt, vanilla, coffee liqueur, and pancake syrup.

3. Blend the ingredients very well.

4. Stir in the chopped pecans and raisins.

5. Pour contents evenly into the pie shell.

6. Bake in preheated 325 degree oven for about 35-45 minutes.

7. Use a knife to check the pie. Insert the knife in the center of the pie. If it comes out clean, you know the pie is finished and ready to eat. Be careful: You might burn your mouth if it is too hot.

(Mary Meow thanks Elinor Soll Cohen, formerly of New Orleans, for this delicious recipe.)

National Standards of Education

This text can be used to supplement any multicultural, interdisciplinary educational setting with a focus on the following National Standards of Education:

Social Sciences Standards > U. S. History > Grades 5-12

o NSS-USH.5-12.2 ERA 2: Colonization and Settlement (1585-1763)

Understands how the values and institutions of European economic life took root in the colonies…

o NSS-USH.5-12.4 ERA 4: Expansion and Reform (1801-1861)

Understands how the industrial revolution, increased immigration, …changed the lives of Americans

Understands the sources and character of cultural…and social reform movements in the antebellum period

Social Science Standards > Geography > Grades K-12

o NSS-G.K.-12.1: The World in Spatial Terms

Understand how to use maps and other geographic representations, … to acquire, process, and report information from a special perspective.

Understand how to use mental maps to organize information about people, places, and environments in a spatial context.

Understand how to analyze the spatial organization of people, places, and environments on Earth's surface.

o NSS-G.K.-12.2: Places and Regions

Understand the physical and human characteristics of places.

Understand that people create regions to interpret Earth's complexity.

Understand how culture and experience influence people's perceptions of places and regions.

o NSS-G.K.-12.4: Human Systems

Understand the characteristics, distribution, and migration of human populations on Earth's surface.

Understand the characteristics, distribution, and complexity of Earth's cultural mosaics.

Understand the patterns and networks of economic interdependence on Earth's surface.

Understand the processes, patterns, and functions of human settlement.

Understand how the forces of cooperation and conflict among people influence the division and control of Earth's surface.

o NSS-G.K-12.5: Environment and Society

Understand how human actions modify the physical environment.

Understand the changes that occur in the meaning, use, distribution, and importance of resources.

Language Arts Standards > English > Grades K-12

o NL-ENG.K-12.1: Reading for Perspective

Students read a wide range of print… to build an understanding of texts, of themselves, and of cultures of the United States and the world….

o NL-ENG.K-12.2: Understanding the Human Experience

Students read a wide range of literature from many periods in many genres to build an understanding of the many dimensions (e.g., philosophical, ethical, aesthetic) of human experience.

o NL-ENG>K-12.3: Evaluation Strategies

Students apply a wide range of strategies to comprehend, interpret, and appreciate texts. They draw on their prior experience, their interactions with other readers and writers, their knowledge of word meaning and of other texts, their word identification strategies, and their understanding of textual features (e.g., sound-letter correspondence, sentence structure, context, graphics).

o NL-ENG.K-12.9: Multicultural Understanding

Students develop an understanding of and respect for diversity in language use, patterns, and dialects across cultures, ethnic groups, geographic regions, and social roles.

Related Web Sites

www.louisianazydecolive.com

www.lafolkroots.org

www.creolehistory.com

www.gensdecouleur.com

www.cajuncultutr.com/other/Zydeco.htm

www.bme.jhu.edu

www.nsula.edu/creole

www.ccet.louisana.edu/cajun_and_Creole_people

www.louisanafolklife.org

www.cajunculture.com

www.yale.edu

www.centralacadianatourism.com

www.louisianarecipes.com

About the Author

Nina J. Haydel, Ed.D.

Dr. Nina Haydel has taught in universities in the USA and abroad since 1984. She is currently academic advisor and professor in the Masters of Arts in Education program in the School of Professional

Education at Central Michigan University. She is also a member of the English Department of Embry-Riddle Aeronautical University, where she teaches numerous online English courses. She retired from public education after 33 years of teaching English and social studies in a Pennsylvania Blue Ribbon high school.

Dr. Haydel has served as an assessment consultant to the National Board for Professional Teaching Standards; evaluator of SAT, GMAT, and Praxis; test item writer for SAT II and CLEP, at ETS, Princeton, NJ; panel member of the National Council for Accreditation of Teacher Education; and

(photo by Elinor Soll Cohen)   consultant/lecturer on curriculum and instruction.

Dr. Haydel taught English composition, American literature, educational strategies and curriculum development in Latin American universities and was visiting professor at the University of Jordan, Amman, Jordan, as well as consultant and lecturer for the Jordanian Ministry of Education. In addition, she served as United States Academic Specialist to Jordan, sponsored by the U. S. State Department. She wrote several television scripts for Jordan TV, about the late King Hussein's impact on his country and on Jordanian education. She has published numerous articles in the field of written composition, online teaching, and educational strategies. As an honorary Creole and the spouse of a Louisiana Creole, she has entered the world of children's literature through her book *Creole Cats Come to Louisiana*.

About the Illustrator

Diane B. Weatherby-Doorman, MA.

Mrs. Doorman has taught art education in public schools for 35 years. She is currently a doctoral student, focusing on brain research. She holds a Masters of Arts in Education and five educational certifications. Mrs. Doorman has been a participant in developing the National Fine and Performing Arts Standards, is an evaluator for the high school proficiency tests, and is a Geraldine Dodge Poet Fellow.